Mystery Bottle

post office

اداره پست

Kristen Balouch

HYPERION BOOKS FOR CHILDREN
NEW YORK

For a boy and his grandfather

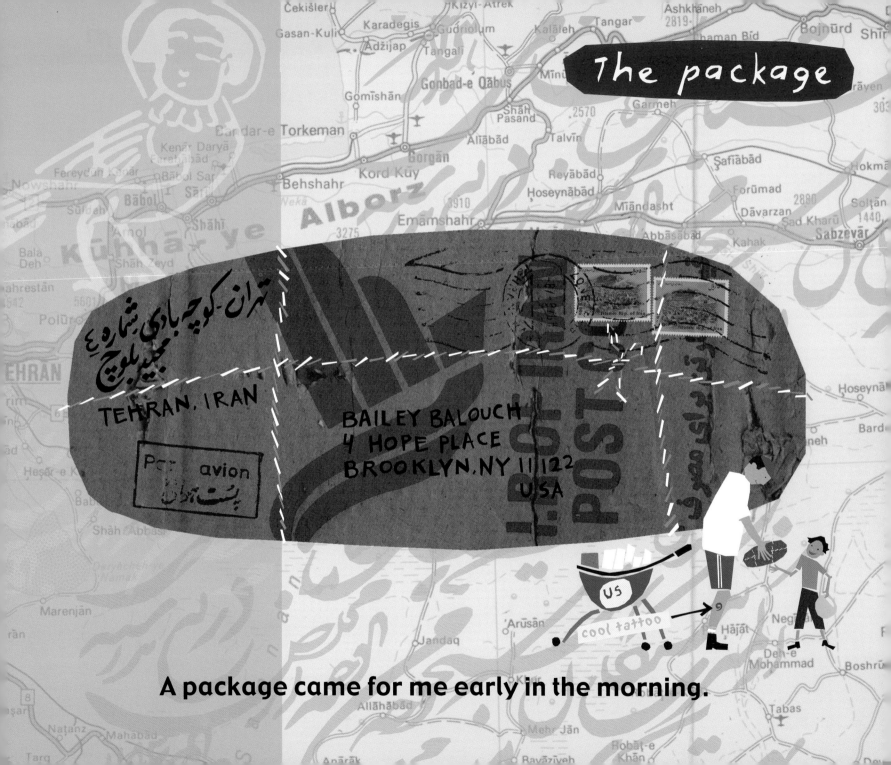

تهران - کوچه بادی شماره ۶
مجید بلوچ

TEHRAN, IRAN

Par avion
پست هوائی

BAILEY BALOUCH
4 HOPE PLACE
BROOKLYN, NY 11122
U.S.A

US

cool tattoo

A package came for me early in the morning.

The bottle

Inside the package was a mysterious little bottle.

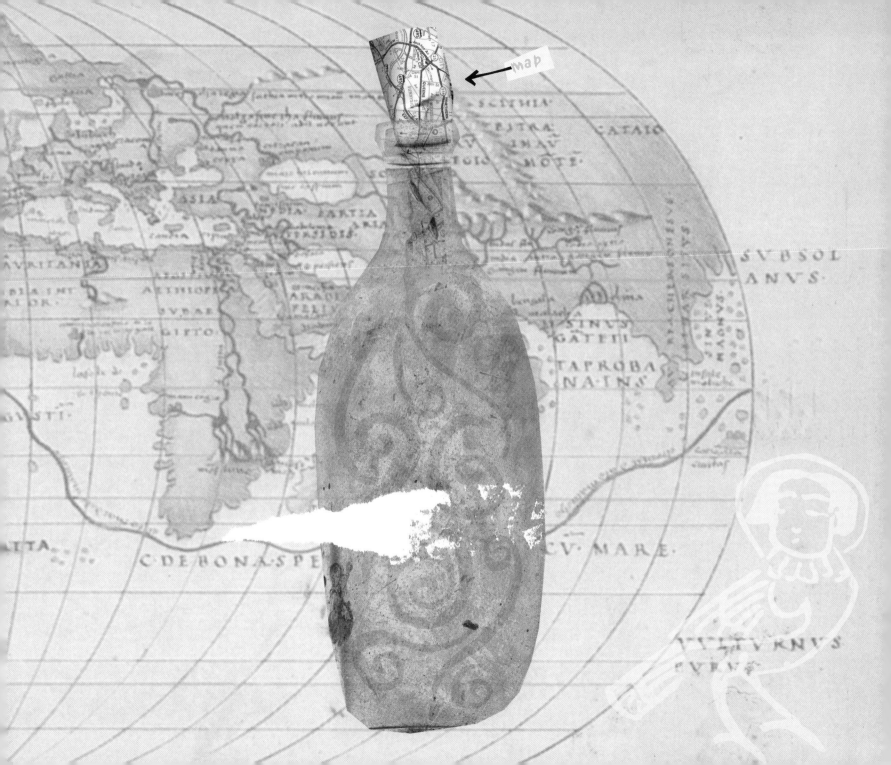

Map

Out of the bottle came a mighty wind, which picked me up and carried me high above the trees and houses.

what a wind

That wind blew me out of the city . . .

The sea

splash

The 'Titanic' largest ship
then afloat sank on her
maiden voyage after striking
an iceberg April 14, 1912.

BERMUDA
(Gt. Br.) → Hamilton
Discovered through shipwreck of
Juan Bermudez early in 16th century.
Dr. William Beebe attained a world
record depth of 3028 feet in 1934.

and across the sea . . .

The mountains

and over tall mountains . . .

The city

and through the city where my father was born . . .

and to the house where my grandfather lives . . .

The arms

ud

tar

setar

squish

bottle collection

. . . and into the arms of my Baba Bozorg.

Tea

What is slimier—a worm or a slug?
What's your favorite color?

my shoes are at the door.

Why are babies born without teeth?

Do you like to make books?

What's your favorite cake?
What do you see without your glasses?
What's more ferocious, a velociraptor or a T. rex?

Is there such a thing as nothing?

How long is forever?
Do you like french fries?
Do you pick apples from trees?

samovar

dolmas

pomegranates

cubes of sugar

We had tea with cubes of sugar
and asked lots of questions.

Did you look like me when you were seven?

I showed Baba Bozorg the empty bottle.
He winked and said, "Come with me."

The mountain

We climbed the tallest mountain.

At the top of the mountain, Baba Bozorg held the empty bottle.

He said, "Breathe in the wind and mix it with love and blow it into the bottle."

The wind

Baba Bozorg gave me a hug, packed the
bottle into my bag, and whispered . . .

The hug

"When you want another cup of tea, just open the bottle, and the wind will bring you to me."

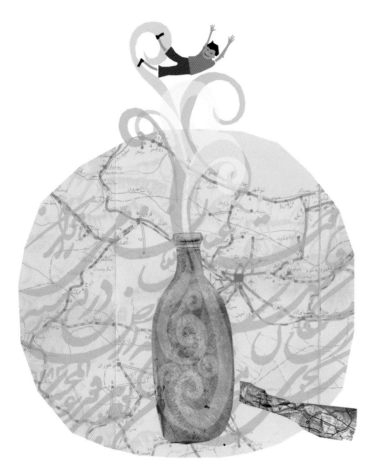

$\mathcal{A}$ father put his boy on an airplane one day in 1978. The boy flew far away, and the father didn't see him. One day the boy called and said he'd gotten married. The father was so happy. But the father didn't see the boy. The boy called again and said his son had been born. The father was so happy. But still the father didn't see the boy. The father waited and waited, and in seven years he sent a package, and the package was addressed to a boy of seven.